For Sam
With love X X X
V.F.

For my dad
S.H.

British Library Cataloguing Publication Data

A catalogue record of this book is available from the British Library

HB ISBN 0 340 77872 5

PB ISBN 0 340 77873 3

First hb edition published 2000

First pb edition published 2000

1 3 5 7 9 10 8 6 4 2

Published by Hodder Children's Books,

a division of Hodder Headline Ltd,

338 Euston Road, London NW1 3BH

Designed by Dawn Apperley

Printed in Hong Kong

Space Dog

Vivian French and Sue Heap

Hodder Children's Books

A division of Hodder Headline Ltd

It was Space Dog's birthday.
Space Dog woke up,
yawned and
stretched.

'Happy Birthday to me!' he said,
and off he *zoomed* into Space.

Space Dog flew up
and up
and up
past the big sun
and the little sun.

'Happy Birthday, Space Dog!'
'Where are you going?' they called.

Space Dog had no time to answer. He flew on . . .

'What's he doing?'
'Where's he going?'
'Happy Birthday, Space Dog!'
called the moons together.

But Space Dog would not stop. He flew on . . .

. . . and on past
the waving wabbits.
'Are you having a party,
Space Dog?' they called.
But Space Dog could not stop. He flew on . . .

. . . and on.

He flew in and out of the **spotty** stars

and the **spotty** stars all sang,

'Happy Birthday to you!'

But Space Dog had no time

even to wag his tail.

Round
and **over**
and **in** and **out**
and **over** once more
and **round** again

flew Space Dog . . .

Home flew Space Dog . . .
back past the **five** spotty stars
and **four** waving wabbits.

Home flew Space Dog . . .
Back past the **three** moons
and **two** suns . . .

Come to

. . . everyone stared at
the words that Space Dog
had written in smoke across the sky.
'Let's party!' said the little sun.

my party

love

from

Space Dog

There are lots of colours in Space.

Blue Moon

Green Moon

and **Purple** Moon

are easy to spot.

What can you

find that is

Yellow

Orange

Green

Black and **White**

and **Red** (with spots!)?